AF230445

NONA VINCENT

AND

THE REAL THING

NONA VINCENT

AND

THE REAL THING

Henry James

PP
Portmay Press
New York

These works by Henry James were originally published in 1892 and are now part of the public domain.

Cover image: Robert Henri, *Young Woman in Black*, 1902. The Art Institute of Chicago.

Published in 2022 by Portmay Press, New York
ISBN 978-1-959986-02-7 (paperback)
ISBN 978-1-959986-03-4 (ebook)

Project management and design by Emily Albarillo

PP

Portmay Press
244 Madison Avenue
New York, NY 10016
www.portmaypress.com

NONA VINCENT

I

"I wondered whether you wouldn't read it to me," said Mrs. Alsager, as they lingered a little near the fire before he took leave. She looked down at the fire sideways, drawing her dress away from it and making her proposal with a shy sincerity that added to her charm. Her charm was always great for Allan Wayworth, and the whole air of her house, which was simply a sort of distillation of herself, so soothing, so beguiling that he always made several false starts before departure. He had spent some such good hours there, had forgotten, in her warm, golden drawing-room, so much of the loneliness and so many of the worries of his life, that it had come to be the immediate answer to his longings, the cure for his aches, the harbor of refuge from his storms. His tribulations were not unprecedented, and some of his advantages, if of a usual kind, were marked in degree, inasmuch as he was very clever for one so young, and very independent for one so poor. He was eight-and-twenty, but he had lived a good deal and was full of ambitions and curiosities and disappointments. The opportunity to talk of some of these in Grosvenor Place corrected perceptibly the immense inconvenience of London. This inconvenience took for him principally the line of insensibility to Allan Wayworth's literary form. He had a literary form, or he thought he had, and her intelligent recognition of the circumstance was the sweetest consolation Mrs. Alsager could have administered. She was even more literary and more artistic than he, inasmuch as he could often work off his overflow (this was his occupation, his profession), while the generous woman, abounding in happy thoughts, but unedited and unpublished, stood there in the rising tide like the nymph of a fountain in the plash of the marble basin.

The year before, in a big newspapery house, he had found himself next her at dinner, and they had converted the intensely material hour into a feast of reason. There was no motive for her asking him to come to see her but that she liked him, which it was the more agreeable to him to perceive as he perceived at the same time that she was exquisite. She was enviably free to act upon her likings, and it made Wayworth feel less unsuccessful to infer that for the moment he happened to be one of them. He kept the revelation to himself, and indeed there was nothing to turn his head in the kindness of a kind woman. Mrs. Alsager occupied so completely the ground of possession that she would have been condemned to inaction had it not been for the principle of giving. Her husband, who was twenty years her senior, a massive personality in the City and a heavy one at home (wherever he stood, or even sat, he was monumental), owned half a big newspaper and the whole of a great many other things. He admired his wife, though she bore no children, and liked her to have other tastes than his, as that seemed to give a greater acreage to their life. His own appetites went so far he could scarcely see the boundary, and his theory was to trust her to push the limits of hers, so that between them the pair should astound by their consumption. His ideas were prodigiously vulgar, but some of them had the good fortune to be carried out by a person of perfect delicacy. Her delicacy made her play strange tricks with them, but he never found this out. She attenuated him without his knowing it, for what he mainly thought was that he had aggrandized *her*. Without her he really would have been bigger still, and society, breathing more freely, was practically under an obligation to her which, to do it justice, it acknowledged by an attitude of mystified respect. She felt a tremulous need to

throw her liberty and her leisure into the things of the soul—
the most beautiful things she knew. She found them, when
she gave time to seeking, in a hundred places, and particularly
in a dim and sacred region—the region of active pity—over
her entrance into which she dropped curtains so thick that
it would have been an impertinence to lift them. But she
cultivated other beneficent passions, and if she cherished
the dream of something fine the moments at which it most
seemed to her to come true were when she saw beauty plucked
flower-like in the garden of art. She loved the perfect work—
she had the artistic chord. This chord could vibrate only to
the touch of another, so that appreciation, in her spirit, had
the added intensity of regret. She could understand the joy
of creation, and she thought it scarcely enough to be told that
she herself created happiness. She would have liked, at any
rate, to choose her way; but it was just here that her liberty
failed her. She had not the voice—she had only the vision.
The only envy she was capable of was directed to those who,
as she said, could do something.

As everything in her, however, turned to gentleness,
she was admirably hospitable to such people as a class. She
believed Allan Wayworth could do something, and she liked
to hear him talk of the ways in which he meant to show
it. He talked of them almost to no one else—she spoiled
him for other listeners. With her fair bloom and her quiet

grace she was indeed an ideal public, and if she had ever confided to him that she would have liked to scribble (she had in fact not mentioned it to a creature), he would have been in a perfect position for asking her why a woman whose face had so much expression should not have felt that she achieved. How in the world could she express better? There was less than that in Shakespeare and Beethoven. She had never been more generous than when, in compliance with her invitation, which I have recorded, he brought his play to read to her. He had spoken of it to her before, and one dark November afternoon, when her red fireside was more than ever an escape from the place and the season, he had broken out as he came in—"I've done it, I've done it!" She made him tell her all about it—she took an interest really minute and asked questions delightfully apt. She had spoken from the first as if he were on the point of being acted, making him jump, with her participation, all sorts of dreary intervals. She liked the theatre as she liked all the arts of expression, and he had known her to go all the way to Paris for a particular performance. Once he had gone with her—the time she took that stupid Mrs. Mostyn. She had been struck, when he sketched it, with the subject of his drama, and had spoken words that helped him to believe in it. As soon as he had rung down his curtain on the last act he rushed off to see her, but after that he kept the thing for repeated last touches. Finally, on Christmas day, by arrangement, she sat there and listened to it. It was in three acts and in prose, but rather of the romantic order, though dealing with contemporary English life, and he fondly believed that it showed the hand if not of the master, at least of the prize pupil.

Allan Wayworth had returned to England, at two-and-twenty, after a miscellaneous continental education; his father, the correspondent, for years, in several foreign countries successively, of a conspicuous London journal, had died just after this, leaving his mother and her two other children, portionless girls, to subsist on a very small income in a very dull German town. The young man's beginnings in London were difficult, and he had aggravated them by his dislike of journalism. His father's connection with it would have helped him, but he was (insanely, most of his friends judged—the great exception was always Mrs. Alsager) *intraitable* on the question of form. Form—in his sense—was not demanded by English newspapers, and he couldn't give it to them in *their* sense. The demand for it was not great anywhere, and Wayworth spent costly weeks in polishing little compositions for magazines that didn't pay for style. The only person who paid for it was really Mrs. Alsager: she had an infallible instinct for the perfect. She paid in her own way, and if Allan Wayworth had been a wage-earning person it would have made him feel that if he didn't receive his legal dues his palm was at least occasionally conscious of a gratuity. He had his limitations, his perversities, but the finest parts of him were the most alive, and he was restless and sincere. It is however the impression he produced on Mrs. Alsager that most concerns us: she thought him not only remarkably good-looking but altogether original. There were some usual bad things he would never do—too many prohibitive puddles for him in the short cut to success.

For himself, he had never been so happy as since he had seen his way, as he fondly believed, to some sort of mastery of the scenic idea, which struck him as a very different matter now that he looked at it from within. He had had his early days of contempt for it, when it seemed to him a jewel, dim at the best, hidden in a dunghill, a taper burning low in an air thick with vulgarity. It was hedged about with sordid approaches, it was not worth sacrifice and suffering. The man of letters, in dealing with it, would have to put off all literature, which was like asking the bearer of a noble name to forego his immemorial heritage. Aspects change, however, with the point of view: Wayworth had waked up one morning in a different bed altogether. It is needless here to trace this accident to its source; it would have been much more interesting to a spectator of the young man's life to follow some of the consequences. He had been made (as he felt) the subject of a special revelation, and he wore his hat like a man in love. An angel had taken him by the hand and guided him to the shabby door which opens, it appeared, into an interior both splendid and austere. The scenic idea was magnificent when once you had embraced it— the dramatic form had a purity which made some others look ingloriously rough. It had the high dignity of the exact sciences, it was mathematical and architectural. It was full of the refreshment of calculation and construction, the incorruptibility of line and law. It was bare, but it was erect, it was poor, but it was noble; it reminded him of some sovereign famed for justice who should have lived in a palace despoiled. There was a fearful amount of concession in it, but what you kept had a rare intensity. You were perpetually throwing over the cargo to save the ship, but what a motion you gave her when you made her ride the waves—a motion as rhythmic as the dance of a goddess! Wayworth took long London walks and thought of these things—London poured into his ears the mighty hum of its suggestion. His imagination glowed and melted down material, his intentions multiplied and made the air a golden haze. He saw not only the thing he should do, but the next and the next and the next; the future opened before him and he seemed to walk on marble slabs. The more he tried the dramatic form the more he loved it, the more he looked at it the more he perceived in it. What he perceived in it indeed he now perceived everywhere; if he stopped, in the London dusk, before some flaring shop-window, the place immediately constituted itself behind footlights, became a framed stage for his figures. He hammered at these figures in his lonely lodging, he shaped them and he shaped their tabernacle; he was like a goldsmith chiseling a casket, bent over with the passion for perfection. When he was neither roaming the streets with his vision nor worrying his problem at his table, he was exchanging ideas on the general question with Mrs. Alsager, to whom he promised details that would amuse her in later and still happier hours. Her eyes were full of tears when he read her the last words of the finished work, and she murmured, divinely—

"And now—to get it done, to get it done!"

"Yes, indeed—to get it done!" Wayworth stared at the fire, slowly rolling up his type-copy. "But that's a totally different part of the business, and altogether secondary."

"But of course you want to be acted?"

"Of course I do—but it's a sudden descent. I want to intensely, but I'm sorry I want to."

"It's there indeed that the difficulties begin," said Mrs. Alsager, a little off her guard.

"How can you say that? It's there that they end!"

"Ah, wait to see where they end!"

"I mean they'll now be of a totally different order," Wayworth explained. "It seems to me there can be nothing in the world more difficult than to write a play that will stand an all-round test, and that in comparison with them the complications that spring up at this point are of an altogether smaller kind."

"Yes, they're not inspiring," said Mrs. Alsager; "they're discouraging, because they're vulgar. The other problem, the working out of the thing itself, is pure art."

"How well you understand everything!" The young man had got up, nervously, and was leaning against the chimney-piece with his back to the fire and his arms folded. The roll of his copy, in his fist, was squeezed into the hollow of one of them. He looked down at Mrs. Alsager, smiling gratefully, and she answered him with a smile from eyes still charmed and suffused. "Yes, the vulgarity will begin now," he presently added.

"You'll suffer dreadfully."

"I shall suffer in a good cause."

"Yes, giving *that* to the world! You must leave it with me, I must read it over and over," Mrs. Alsager pleaded, rising to come nearer and draw the copy, in its cover of greenish-gray paper, which had a generic identity now to him, out of his grasp. "Who in the world will do it?—who in the world *can?*" she went on, close to him, turning over the leaves. Before he could answer she had stopped at one of the pages; she turned the book round to him, pointing out a speech. "That's the most beautiful place—those lines are a perfection." He glanced at the spot she indicated, and she begged him to read them again—he had read them admirably before. He knew them by heart, and, closing the book while she held the other end of it, he murmured them over to her—they had indeed a cadence that pleased him—watching, with a facetious complacency which he hoped was pardonable, the applause in her face. "Ah, who can utter such lines as *that?*" Mrs. Alsager broke out; "whom can you find to do *her?*"

"We'll find people to do them all!"

"But not people who are worthy."

"They'll be worthy enough if they're willing enough. I'll work with them—I'll grind it into them." He spoke as if he had produced twenty plays.

"Oh, it will be interesting!" she echoed.

"But I shall have to find my theatre first. I shall have to get a manager to believe in me."

"Yes—they're so stupid!"

"But fancy the patience I shall want, and how I shall have to watch and wait," said Allan Wayworth. "Do you see me hawking it about London?"

"Indeed I don't—it would be sickening."

"It's what I shall have to do. I shall be old before it's produced."

"I shall be old very soon if it isn't!" Mrs. Alsager cried. "I know one or two of them," she mused.

"Do you mean you would speak to them?"

"The thing is to get them to read it. I could do that."

"That's the utmost I ask. But it's even for that I shall have to wait."

She looked at him with kind sisterly eyes. "You sha'n't wait."

"Ah, you dear lady!" Wayworth murmured.

"That is *you* may, but *I* won't! Will you leave me your copy?" she went on, turning the pages again.

"Certainly; I have another." Standing near him she read to herself a passage here and there; then, in her sweet voice, she read some of them out. "Oh, if *you* were only an actress!" the young man exclaimed.

"That's the last thing I am. There's no comedy in *me*!"

She had never appeared to Wayworth so much his good genius. "Is there any tragedy?" he asked, with the levity of complete confidence.

She turned away from him, at this, with a strange and charming laugh and a "Perhaps that will be for you to determine!" But before he could disclaim such a responsibility she had faced him again and was talking about Nona Vincent as if she had been the most interesting of their friends and her situation at that moment an irresistible appeal to their sympathy. Nona Vincent was the heroine of the play, and Mrs. Alsager had taken a tremendous fancy to her. "I can't *tell* you how I like that woman!" she exclaimed in a pensive rapture of credulity which could only be balm to the artistic spirit.

"I'm awfully glad she lives a bit. What I feel about her is that she's a good deal like *you*," Wayworth observed.

Mrs. Alsager stared an instant and turned faintly red. This was evidently a view that failed to strike her; she didn't, however, treat it as a joke. "I'm not impressed with the resemblance. I don't see myself doing what she does."

"It isn't so much what she *does*," the young man argued, drawing out his moustache.

"But what she does is the whole point. She simply tells her love—I should never do that."

"If you repudiate such a proceeding with such energy, why do you like her for it?"

"It isn't what I like her for."

"What else, then? That's intensely characteristic."

Mrs. Alsager reflected, looking down at the fire; she had the air of having half-a-dozen reasons to choose from. But the one she produced was unexpectedly simple; it might even have been prompted by despair at not finding others. "I like her because *you* made her!" she exclaimed with a laugh, moving again away from her companion.

Wayworth laughed still louder. "You made her a little yourself. I've thought of her as looking like you."

"She ought to look much better," said Mrs. Alsager. "No, certainly, I shouldn't do what *she* does."

"Not even in the same circumstances?"

"I should never find myself in such circumstances. They're exactly your play, and have nothing in common with such a life as mine. However," Mrs. Alsager went on, "her behavior was natural for *her*, and not only natural, but, it seems to me, thoroughly beautiful and noble. I can't sufficiently admire the talent and tact with which you make one accept it, and I tell you frankly that it's evident to me there must be a brilliant future before a young man who, at the start, has been capable of such a stroke as that. Thank heaven I can admire Nona Vincent as intensely as I feel that I don't resemble her!"

"Don't exaggerate that," said Allan Wayworth.

"My admiration?"

"Your dissimilarity. She has your face, your air, your voice, your motion; she has many elements of your being."

"Then she'll damn your play!" Mrs. Alsager replied. They joked a little over this, though it was not in the tone of pleasantry that Wayworth's hostess soon remarked: "You've got your remedy, however: have her done by the right woman."

"Oh, have her 'done'—have her 'done'!" the young man gently wailed.

"I see what you mean, my poor friend. What a pity, when

it's such a magnificent part—such a chance for a clever serious girl! Nona Vincent is practically your play—it will be open to her to carry it far or to drop it at the first corner."

"It's a charming prospect," said Allan Wayworth, with sudden skepticism. They looked at each other with eyes that, for a lurid moment, saw the worst of the worst; but before they parted they had exchanged vows and confidences that were dedicated wholly to the ideal. It is not to be supposed, however, that the knowledge that Mrs. Alsager would help him made Wayworth less eager to help himself. He did what he could and felt that she, on her side, was doing no less; but at the end of a year he was obliged to recognize that their united effort had mainly produced the fine flower of discouragement. At the end of a year the luster had, to his own eyes, quite faded from his unappreciated masterpiece, and he found him-self writing for a biographical dictionary little lives of celebri-ties he had never heard of. To be printed, anywhere and any-how, was a form of glory for a man so unable to be acted, and to be paid, even at encyclopedic rates, had the consequence of making one resigned and verbose. He couldn't smuggle style into a dictionary, but he could at least reflect that he had done his best to learn from the drama that it is a gross imperti-nence almost anywhere. He had knocked at the door of every theatre in London, and, at a ruinous expense, had multiplied type-copies of *Nona Vincent* to replace the neat transcripts that had descended into the managerial abyss. His play was not even declined—no such flattering intimation was given him that it had been read. What the managers would do for Mrs. Alsager concerned him little today; the thing that was relevant was that they would do nothing for *him*. That charming woman felt humbled to the earth, so little response had she had from the powers on which she counted. The two never talked about the play now, but he tried to show her a still finer friendship, that she might not think he felt she had failed him. He still walked about London with his dreams, but as months succeeded months and he left the year behind him they were dreams not so much of success as of revenge. Success seemed a colorless name for the reward of his patience; something fiercely florid, something sanguinolent was more to the point. His best consolation however was still in the scenic idea; it was not till now that he discovered how incurably he was in love with it. By the time a vain second year had chafed itself away he cherished his fruitless faculty the more for the obloquy it seemed to suffer. He lived, in his best hours, in a world of subjects and situations; he wrote another play and made it as different from its predecessor as such a very good thing could be. It might be a very good thing, but when he had committed it to the theatrical limbo indiscriminating fate took no account of the difference. He was at last able to leave England for three or four months; he went to Germany to pay a visit long deferred to his mother and sisters.

Shortly before the time he had fixed for his return he received from Mrs. Alsager a telegram consisting of the words: "Loder wishes see you—putting *Nona* instant rehearsal." He spent the few hours before his departure in kissing his mother and sisters, who knew enough about Mrs. Alsager to judge it lucky this respectable married lady was not there—a relief, however, accompanied with speculative glances at London and the morrow. Loder, as our young man was aware, meant the new "Renaissance," but though he reached home in the evening it was not to this convenient modern theatre that Wayworth first proceeded. He spent a late hour with Mrs. Alsager, an hour that throbbed with calculation. She told him that Mr. Loder was charming, he had simply taken up the play in its turn; he had hopes of it, moreover, that on the part of a professional pessimist might almost be qualified as ecstatic. It had been cast, with a margin for objections, and Violet Grey was to do the heroine. She had been capable, while he was away, of a good piece of work at that foggy old playhouse the "Legitimate;" the piece was a clumsy *réchauffé*, but she at least had been fresh. Wayworth remembered Violet Grey— hadn't he, for two years, on a fond policy of "looking out," kept dipping into the London theatres to pick up prospective interpreters? He had not picked up many as yet, and this young lady at all events had never wriggled in his net. She was pretty and she was odd, but he had never prefigured her as Nona Vincent, nor indeed found himself attracted by what he already felt sufficiently launched in the profession to speak of as her artistic personality. Mrs. Alsager was different—she declared that she had been struck not a little by some of her tones. The girl was interesting in the thing at the "Legitimate," and Mr. Loder, who had his eye on her, described her as ambitious and intelligent. She wanted awfully to get on—and some of those ladies were so lazy! Wayworth was skeptical— he had seen Miss Violet Grey, who was terribly itinerant, in a dozen theatres but only in one aspect. Nona Vincent had a dozen aspects, but only one theatre; yet with what a feverish curiosity the young man promised himself to watch the actress on the morrow! Talking the matter over with Mrs. Alsager now seemed the very stuff that rehearsal was made of. The near prospect of being acted laid a finger even on the lip of inquiry; he wanted to go on tiptoe till the first night, to make no condition but that they should speak his lines, and he felt that he wouldn't so much as raise an eyebrow at the scene-painter if he should give him an old oak chamber.

He became conscious, the next day, that his danger would be other than this, and yet he couldn't have expressed to himself what it would be. Danger was there, doubtless— danger was everywhere, in the world of art, and still more in the world of commerce; but what he really seemed to catch, for the hour, was the beating of the wings of victory. Nothing could undermine that, since it was victory simply to be acted. It would be victory even to be acted badly; a reflection that didn't prevent him, however, from banishing, in his politic optimism, the word "bad" from his vocabulary. It had no application, in the compromise of practice; it didn't apply even to his play, which he was conscious he had already outlived and as to which he foresaw that, in the coming weeks, frequent alarm would alternate, in his spirit, with frequent esteem. When he went down to the dusky daylit theatre (it arched over him like the temple of fame) Mr. Loder, who was as charming as Mrs. Alsager had announced, struck him as the genius of hospitality. The manager began to explain why, for so long, he had given no sign; but that was the last thing that interested Wayworth now, and he could never remember afterwards what reasons Mr. Loder had enumerated. He liked, in the whole business of discussion and preparation, even the things he had thought he should probably dislike, and he reveled in those he had thought he should like. He watched Miss Violet Grey that evening with eyes that sought to penetrate her possibilities. She certainly had a few; they were qualities of voice and face, qualities perhaps even of intelligence; he sat there at any rate with a fostering, coaxing attention, repeating over to himself as convincingly as he could that she was not common—a circumstance all the more creditable as the part she was playing seemed to him desperately so. He perceived that this was why it pleased the audience; he divined that it was the part they enjoyed rather than the actress. He had a private panic, wondering how, if they liked *that* form, they could possibly like his. His form had now become quite an ultimate idea to him. By the time the evening was over some of Miss Violet Grey's features, several of the turns of her head, a certain vibration of her voice, had taken their place in the same category. She *was* interesting, she was distinguished; at any rate he had accepted her: it came to the same thing. But he left the theatre that night without speaking to her—moved (a little even to his own mystification) by an odd procrastinating impulse. On the morrow he was to read his three acts to the company, and then he should have a good deal to say; what he felt for the moment was a vague indisposition to commit himself. Moreover he found a slight confusion of annoyance in the fact that though he had been trying all the evening to look at Nona Vincent in Violet Grey's person, what subsisted in his vision was simply Violet Grey in Nona's. He didn't wish to see the actress so directly, or even so simply as that; and it had been very fatiguing, the effort to focus Nona both through the performer and through the "Legitimate." Before he went to bed that night he posted three words to Mrs. Alsager—"She's not a bit like it, but I dare say I can make her do."

He was pleased with the way the actress listened, the next day, at the reading; he was pleased indeed with many things, at the reading, and most of all with the reading itself. The whole affair loomed large to him and he magnified it and mapped it out. He enjoyed his occupation of the big, dim, hollow theatre, full of the echoes of "effect" and of a queer smell of gas and success—it all seemed such a passive canvas for his picture. For the first time in his life he was in command of resources; he was acquainted with the phrase, but had never thought he should know the feeling. He was surprised at what Loder appeared ready to do, though he reminded himself that he must never show it. He foresaw that there would be two distinct concomitants to the artistic effort of producing a play, one consisting of a great deal of anguish and the other of a great deal of amusement. He looked back upon the reading, afterwards, as the best hour in the business, because it was then that the piece had most struck him as represented. What came later was the doing of others; but this, with its imperfections and failures, was all his own. The drama lived, at any rate, for that hour, with an intensity that it was promptly to lose in the poverty and patchiness of rehearsal; he could see its life reflected, in a way that was sweet to him, in the stillness of the little semi-circle of attentive and inscrutable, of water-proofed and muddy-booted, actors. Miss Violet Grey was the auditor he had most to say to, and he tried on the spot, across the shabby stage, to let her have the soul of her part. Her attitude was graceful, but though she appeared to listen with all her faculties her face remained perfectly blank; a fact, however, not discouraging to Wayworth, who liked her better for not being premature. Her companions gave discernible signs of recognizing the passages of comedy; yet Wayworth forgave her even then for being inexpressive. She evidently wished before everything else to be simply sure of what it was all about.

He was more surprised even than at the revelation of the scale on which Mr. Loder was ready to proceed by the discovery that some of the actors didn't like their parts, and his heart sank as he asked himself what he could possibly do with them if they were going to be so stupid. This was the first of his disappointments; somehow he had expected every individual to become instantly and gratefully conscious of a rare opportunity, and from the moment such a calculation failed he was at sea, or mindful at any rate that more disappointments would come. It was impossible to make out what the manager liked or disliked; no judgment, no comment escaped him; his acceptance of the play and his views about the way it should be mounted had apparently converted him into a veiled and shrouded figure. Wayworth was able to grasp the idea that they would all move now in a higher and sharper air than that of compliment and confidence. When he talked with Violet Grey after the reading he gathered that she was really rather crude: what better proof of it could there be than her failure to break out instantly with an expression of delight about her great chance? This reserve, however, had evidently nothing to do with high pretensions; she had no wish to make him feel that a person of her eminence was superior to easy raptures. He guessed, after a little, that she was puzzled and even somewhat frightened—to a certain extent she had not understood. Nothing could appeal to him more than the opportunity to clear up her difficulties, in the course of the examination of which he quickly discovered that, so far as she *had* understood, she had understood wrong. If she was crude it was only a reason the more for talking to her; he kept saying to her "Ask me—ask me: ask me everything you can think of."

She asked him, she was perpetually asking him, and at the first rehearsals, which were without form and void to a degree that made them strike him much more as the death of an experiment than as the dawn of a success, they threshed things out immensely in a corner of the stage, with the effect of his coming to feel that at any rate she was in earnest. He felt more and more that his heroine was the keystone of his arch, for which indeed the actress was very ready to take her. But when he reminded this young lady of the way the whole thing practically depended on her she was alarmed and even slightly scandalized: she spoke more than once as if that could scarcely be the right way to construct a play—make it stand or fall by one poor nervous girl. She was almost morbidly conscientious, and in theory he liked her for this, though he lost patience three or four times with the things she couldn't do and the things she could. At such times the tears came to her eyes; but they were produced by her own stupidity, she hastened to assure him, not by the way he spoke, which was awfully kind under the circumstances. Her sincerity made her beautiful, and he wished to heaven (and made a point of telling her so) that she could sprinkle a little of it over Nona. Once, however, she was so touched and troubled that the sight of it brought the tears for an instant to his own eyes; and it so happened that, turning at this moment, he found himself face to face with Mr. Loder. The manager stared, glanced at the actress, who turned in the other direction, and then smiling at Wayworth, exclaimed, with the humor of a man who heard the gallery laugh every night:

"I say—I say!"

"What's the matter?" Wayworth asked.

"I'm glad to see Miss Grey is taking such pains with you."

"Oh, yes—she'll turn me out!" said the young man, gaily. He was quite aware that it was apparent he was not superficial about Nona, and abundantly determined, into the bargain, that the rehearsal of the piece should not sacrifice a shade of thoroughness to any extrinsic consideration.

Mrs. Alsager, whom, late in the afternoon, he used often to go and ask for a cup of tea, thanking her in advance for the rest she gave him and telling her how he found that rehearsal (as *they* were doing it—it was a caution!) took it out of one—Mrs. Alsager, more and more his good genius and, as he repeatedly assured her, his ministering angel, confirmed him in this superior policy and urged him on to every form of artistic devotion. She had, naturally, never been more interested than now in his work; she wanted to hear everything about everything. She treated him as heroically fatigued, plied him with luxurious restoratives, made him stretch himself on cushions and rose-leaves. They gossiped more than ever, by her fire, about the artistic life; he confided to her, for instance, all his hopes and fears, all his experiments and anxieties, on the subject of the representative of Nona. She was immensely interested in this young lady and showed it by taking a box again and again (she had seen her half-a-dozen times already), to study her capacity through the veil of her present part. Like Allan Wayworth she found her encouraging only by fits, for she had fine flashes of badness.

She was intelligent, but she cried aloud for training, and the training was so absent that the intelligence had only a fraction of its effect. She was like a knife without an edge—good steel that had never been sharpened; she hacked away at her hard dramatic loaf, she couldn't cut it smooth.

II

"Certainly my leading lady won't make Nona much like *you!*" Wayworth one day gloomily remarked to Mrs. Alsager. There were days when the prospect seemed to him awful.

"So much the better. There's no necessity for that."

"I wish you'd train her a little—you could so easily," the young man went on; in response to which Mrs. Alsager requested him not to make such cruel fun of her. But she was curious about the girl, wanted to hear of her character, her private situation, how she lived and where, seemed indeed desirous to befriend her. Wayworth might not have known much about the private situation of Miss Violet Grey, but, as it happened, he was able, by the time his play had been three weeks in rehearsal, to supply information on such points. She was a charming, exemplary person, educated, cultivated, with highly modern tastes, an excellent musician. She had lost her parents and was very much alone in the world, her only two relations being a sister, who was married to a civil servant (in a highly responsible post) in India, and a dear little old-fashioned aunt (really a great-aunt) with whom she lived at Notting Hill, who wrote children's books and who, it appeared, had once written a Christmas pantomime. It was quite an artistic home—not on the scale of Mrs. Alsager's (to compare the smallest things with the greatest!) but intensely refined and honorable. Wayworth went so far as to hint that it would be rather nice and human on Mrs. Alsager's part to go there—they would take it so kindly if she should call on them. She had acted so often on his hints that he had formed a pleasant habit of expecting it: it made him feel so wisely responsible about giving them. But this one appeared to fall to the ground, so that he let the subject drop. Mrs. Alsager, however, went yet once more to the "Legitimate," as he found by her saying to him abruptly, on the morrow: "Oh, she'll be very good—she'll be very good." When they said "she," in these days, they always meant Violet Grey, though they pretended, for the most part, that they meant Nona Vincent.

"Oh yes," Wayworth assented, "she wants so to!"

Mrs. Alsager was silent a moment; then she asked, a little inconsequently, as if she had come back from a reverie: "Does she want to *very* much?"

"Tremendously—and it appears she has been fascinated by the part from the first."

"Why then didn't she say so?"

"Oh, because she's so funny."

"She *is* funny," said Mrs. Alsager, musingly; and presently she added: "She's in love with you."

Wayworth stared, blushed very red, then laughed out. "What is there funny in that?" he demanded; but before his interlocutress could satisfy him on this point he inquired, further, how she knew anything about it. After a little graceful evasion she explained that the night before, at the "Legitimate," Mrs. Beaumont, the wife of the actor-manager, had paid her a visit in her box; which had happened, in the course of their brief gossip, to lead to her remarking that she had never been "behind." Mrs. Beaumont offered on the spot to take her round, and the fancy had seized her to accept the invitation. She had been amused for the moment, and in this way it befell that her conductress, at her request, had introduced her to Miss Violet Grey, who was waiting in the wing for one of her scenes. Mrs. Beaumont had been called away for three minutes, and during this scrap of time, face to face with the actress, she had discovered the poor girl's secret. Wayworth qualified it as a senseless thing, but wished to know what had led to the discovery. She characterized this inquiry as superficial for a painter of the ways of women; and he doubtless didn't improve it by remarking profanely that a cat might look at a king and that such things were convenient to know. Even on this ground, however, he was threatened by Mrs. Alsager, who contended that it might not be a joking matter to the poor girl. To this Wayworth, who now professed to hate talking about the passions he might have inspired, could only reply that he meant it couldn't make a difference to Mrs. Alsager.

"How in the world do you know what makes a difference to *me?*" this lady asked, with incongruous coldness, with a haughtiness indeed remarkable in so gentle a spirit.

He saw Violet Grey that night at the theatre, and it was she who spoke first of her having lately met a friend of his.

"She's in love with you," the actress said, after he had made a show of ignorance; "doesn't that tell you anything?"

He blushed redder still than Mrs. Alsager had made him blush, but replied, quickly enough and very adequately, that hundreds of women were naturally dying for him.

"Oh, I don't care, for you're not in love with *her!*" the girl continued.

"Did she tell you that too?" Wayworth asked; but she had at that moment to go on.

Standing where he could see her he thought that on this occasion she threw into her scene, which was the best she had in the play, a brighter art than ever before, a talent that could play with its problem. She was perpetually doing things out of rehearsal (she did two or three tonight, in the other man's piece), that he as often wished to heaven Nona Vincent might have the benefit of. She appeared to be able to do them for every one but him—that is for every one but Nona. He was conscious, in these days, of an odd new feeling, which mixed (this was a part of its oddity) with a very natural and comparatively old one and which in its most definite form was a dull ache of regret that this young lady's unlucky star should have placed her on the stage. He wished in his worst uneasiness that, without going further, she would give it up; and yet it soothed that uneasiness to remind himself that he saw grounds to hope she would go far enough to make a marked success of Nona. There were strange and painful moments when, as the interpretress of Nona, he almost hated her; after which, however, he always assured himself that he exaggerated, inasmuch as what made this aversion seem great, when he was nervous, was simply its contrast with the growing sense that there *were* grounds—totally different—on which she pleased him. She pleased him as a charming creature—by her sincerities and her perversities, by the varieties and surprises of her character and by certain happy facts of her person. In private her eyes were sad to him and her voice was rare. He detested the idea that she should have a disappointment or an humiliation, and he wanted to rescue her altogether, to save and transplant her. One way to save her was to see to it, to the best of his ability, that the production of his play should be a triumph; and the other way—it was really too queer to express—was almost to wish that it shouldn't be. Then, for the future, there would be safety and peace, and not the peace of death—the peace of a different life. It is to be added that our young man clung to the former of these ways in proportion as the latter perversely tempted him. He was nervous at the best, increasingly and intolerably nervous; but the immediate remedy was to rehearse harder and harder, and above all to work it out with Violet Grey. Some of her comrades reproached him with working it out only with her, as if she were the whole affair; to which he replied that they could afford to be neglected, they were all so tremendously good. She was the only person concerned whom he didn't flatter.

The author and the actress stuck so to the business in hand that she had very little time to speak to him again of Mrs. Alsager, of whom indeed her imagination appeared adequately to have disposed. Wayworth once remarked to her that Nona Vincent was supposed to be a good deal like his charming friend; but she gave a blank "Supposed by whom?" in consequence of which he never returned to the subject. He confided his nervousness as freely as usual to Mrs. Alsager, who easily understood that he had a peculiar complication of anxieties. His suspense varied in degree from hour to hour, but any relief there might have been in this was made up for by its being of several different kinds. One afternoon, as the first performance drew near, Mrs. Alsager said to him, in giving him his cup of tea and on his having mentioned that he had not closed his eyes the night before:

"You must indeed be in a dreadful state. Anxiety for another is still worse than anxiety for one's self."

"For another?" Wayworth repeated, looking at her over the rim of his cup.

"My poor friend, you're nervous about Nona Vincent, but you're infinitely more nervous about Violet Grey."

"She *is* Nona Vincent!"

"No, she isn't—not a bit!" said Mrs. Alsager, abruptly.

"Do you really think so?" Wayworth cried, spilling his tea in his alarm.

"What I think doesn't signify—I mean what I think about that. What I meant to say was that great as is your suspense about your play, your suspense about your actress is greater still."

"I can only repeat that my actress *is* my play."

Mrs. Alsager looked thoughtfully into the teapot.

"Your actress is your—"

"My what?" the young man asked, with a little tremor in his voice, as his hostess paused.

"Your very dear friend. You're in love with her—at present." And with a sharp click Mrs. Alsager dropped the lid on the fragrant receptacle.

"Not yet—not yet!" laughed her visitor.

"You will be if she pulls you through."

"You declare that she *won't* pull me through."

Mrs. Alsager was silent a moment, after which she softly murmured: "I'll pray for her."

"You're the most generous of women!" Wayworth cried; then colored as if the words had not been happy. They would have done indeed little honor to a man of tact.

The next morning he received five hurried lines from Mrs. Alsager. She had suddenly been called to Torquay, to see a relation who was seriously ill; she should be detained there several days, but she had an earnest hope of being able to return in time for his first night. In any event he had her unrestricted good wishes. He missed her extremely, for these last days were a great strain and there was little comfort to be derived from Violet Grey. She was even more nervous than himself, and so pale and altered that he was afraid she would be too ill to act. It was settled between them that they made each other worse and that he had now much better leave her alone. They had pulled Nona so to pieces that nothing seemed left of her—she must at least have time to grow together again. He left Violet Grey alone, to the best of his ability, but she carried out imperfectly her own side of the bargain. She came to him with new questions—she waited for him with old doubts, and half an hour before the last dress-rehearsal, on the eve of production, she proposed to him a totally fresh rendering of his heroine. This incident gave him such a sense of insecurity that he turned his back on her without a word, bolted out of the theatre, dashed along the Strand and walked as far as the Bank. Then he jumped into a hansom and came westward, and when he reached the theatre again the business was nearly over. It appeared, almost to his disappointment, not bad enough to give him the consolation of the old playhouse adage that the worst dress-rehearsals make the best first nights.

The morrow, which was a Wednesday, was the dreadful day; the theatre had been closed on the Monday and the Tuesday. Every one, on the Wednesday, did his best to let every one else alone, and every one signally failed in the attempt. The day, till seven o'clock, was understood to be consecrated to rest, but every one except Violet Grey turned up at the theatre. Wayworth looked at Mr. Loder, and Mr.

Loder looked in another direction, which was as near as they came to conversation. Wayworth was in a fidget, unable to eat or sleep or sit still, at times almost in terror. He kept quiet by keeping, as usual, in motion; he tried to walk away from his nervousness. He walked in the afternoon toward Notting Hill, but he succeeded in not breaking the vow he had taken not to meddle with his actress. She was like an acrobat poised on a slippery ball—if he should touch her she would topple over. He passed her door three times and he thought of her three hundred. This was the hour at which he most regretted that Mrs. Alsager had not come back—for he had called at her house only to learn that she was still at Torquay. This was probably queer, and it was probably queerer still that she hadn't written to him; but even of these things he wasn't sure, for in losing, as he had now completely lost, his judgment of his play, he seemed to himself to have lost his judgment of everything. When he went home, however, he found a telegram from the lady of Grosvenor Place—"Shall be able to come—reach town by seven." At half-past eight o'clock, through a little aperture in the curtain of the "Renaissance," he saw her in her box with a cluster of friends—completely beautiful and beneficent. The house was magnificent—too good for his play, he felt; too good for any play. Everything now seemed too good— the scenery, the furniture, the dresses, the very programs. He seized upon the idea that this was probably what was the matter with the representative of Nona—she was only too good. He had completely arranged with this young lady the plan of their relations during the evening; and though they had altered everything else that they had arranged they had promised each other not to alter this. It was wonderful the number of things they had promised each other. He would start her, he would see her off—then he would quit the theatre and stay away till just before the end. She besought him to stay away—it would make her infinitely easier. He saw that she was exquisitely dressed—she had made one or two changes for the better since the night before, and that seemed something definite to turn over and over in his mind as he rumbled foggily home in the four-wheeler in which, a few steps from the stage-door, he had taken refuge as soon as he knew that the curtain was up. He lived a couple of miles off, and he had chosen a four-wheeler to drag out the time.

When he got home his fire was out, his room was cold, and he lay down on his sofa in his overcoat. He had sent his landlady to the dress-circle, on purpose; she would overflow with words and mistakes. The house seemed a black void, just as the streets had done—every one was, formidably, at his play. He was quieter at last than he had been for a fortnight, and he felt too weak even to wonder how the thing was going. He believed afterwards that he had slept an hour; but even if he had he felt it to be still too early to return to the theatre. He sat down by his lamp and tried to read—to read a little compendious life of a great English statesman, out of a "series." It struck him as brilliantly clever, and he asked himself whether that perhaps were not rather the sort of thing he ought to have taken up: not the statesmanship, but the art of brief biography. Suddenly he became aware that he must hurry if he was to reach the theatre at all—it was a quarter to eleven o'clock. He scrambled out and, this time, found a hansom—he had lately spent enough money in cabs to add to his hope that the profits of his new profession would be great. His anxiety, his suspense flamed up again, and as he rattled eastward—he went fast now—he was almost sick with alternations. As he passed into the theatre the first man—some underling—who met him, cried to him, breathlessly:

"You're wanted, sir—you're wanted!" He thought his tone very ominous—he devoured the man's eyes with his own, for a betrayal: did he mean that he was wanted for execution? Some one else pressed him, almost pushed him, forward; he was already on the stage. Then he became conscious of a sound more or less continuous, but seemingly faint and far, which he took at first for the voice of the actors heard through their canvas walls, the beautiful built-in room of the last act. But the actors were in the wing, they surrounded him; the curtain was down and they were coming off from before it. They had been called, and *he* was called—they all greeted him with "Go on—go on!" He was terrified—he couldn't go on—he didn't believe in the applause, which seemed to him only audible enough to sound half-hearted.

"Has it gone?—*has* it gone?" he gasped to the people round him; and he heard them say "Rather—rather!" perfunctorily, mendaciously too, as it struck him, and even with mocking laughter, the laughter of defeat and despair. Suddenly, though all this must have taken but a moment, Loder burst upon him from somewhere with a "For God's sake don't keep them, or they'll *stop!*" "But I can't go on for *that!*" Wayworth cried, in anguish; the sound seemed to him already to have ceased. Loder had hold of him and was shoving him; he resisted and looked round frantically for Violet Grey, who perhaps would tell him the truth. There was by this time a crowd in the wing, all with strange grimacing painted faces, but Violet was not among them and her very absence frightened him. He uttered her name with an accent that he afterwards regretted—it gave them, as he thought, both away; and while Loder hustled him before the curtain he heard some one say "She took her call and disappeared." She had had a call, then—this was what was most present to the young man as he stood for an instant in the glare of the footlights, looking blindly at the great vaguely-peopled horseshoe and greeted with plaudits which now seemed to him at once louder than he deserved and feebler than he desired. They sank to rest quickly, but he felt it to be long before he could back away, before he could, in his turn, seize the manager by the arm and cry huskily—"Has it really gone—*really?*"

Mr. Loder looked at him hard and replied after an instant: "The play's all right!"

Wayworth hung upon his lips. "Then what's all wrong?"

"We must do something to Miss Grey."

"What's the matter with her?"

"She isn't *in* it!"

"Do you mean she has failed?"

"Yes, damn it—she has failed."

Wayworth stared. "Then how can the play be all right?"

"Oh, we'll save it—we'll save it."

"Where's Miss Grey—where *is* she?" the young man asked.

Loder caught his arm as he was turning away again to look for his heroine. "Never mind her now—she knows it!"

Wayworth was approached at the same moment by a gentleman he knew as one of Mrs. Alsager's friends—he had perceived him in that lady's box. Mrs. Alsager was waiting there for the successful author; she desired very earnestly that he would come round and speak to her. Wayworth assured himself first that Violet had left the theatre—one of the actresses could tell him that she had seen her throw on a cloak, without changing her dress, and had learnt afterwards that she had, the next moment, flung herself, after flinging her aunt, into a cab. He had wished to invite half a dozen persons, of whom Miss Grey and her elderly relative were two, to come home to supper with him; but she had refused to make any engagement beforehand (it would be so dreadful to have to keep it if she shouldn't have made a hit), and this attitude had blighted the pleasant plan, which fell to the ground. He had called her morbid, but she was immovable. Mrs. Alsager's messenger let him know that he was expected to supper in Grosvenor Place, and half an hour afterwards he was seated there among complimentary people and flowers and popping corks, eating the first orderly meal he had partaken of for a week. Mrs. Alsager had carried him off in her brougham—the other people who were coming got into things of their own. He stopped her short as soon as she began to tell him how tremendously every one had been struck by the piece; he nailed her down to the question of Violet Grey. Had she spoiled the play, had she jeopardized or compromised it—had she been utterly bad, had she been good in any degree?

"Certainly the performance would have seemed better if *she* had been better," Mrs. Alsager confessed.

"And the play would have seemed better if the performance had been better," Wayworth said, gloomily, from the corner of the brougham.

"She does what she can, and she has talent, and she looked lovely. But she doesn't *see* Nona Vincent. She doesn't see the type—she doesn't see the individual—she doesn't see the woman you meant. She's out of it—she gives you a different person."

"Oh, the woman I meant!" the young man exclaimed, looking at the London lamps as he rolled by them. "I wish to God she had known *you!*" he added, as the carriage stopped. After they had passed into the house he said to his companion:

"You see she *won't* pull me through."

"Forgive her—be kind to her!" Mrs. Alsager pleaded.

"I shall only thank her. The play may go to the dogs."

"If it does—if it does," Mrs. Alsager began, with her pure eyes on him.

"Well, what if it does?"

She couldn't tell him, for the rest of her guests came in together; she only had time to say: "It *sha'n't* go to the dogs!"

He came away before the others, restless with the desire to go to Notting Hill even that night, late as it was, haunted with the sense that Violet Grey had measured her fall. When he got into the street, however, he allowed second thoughts to counsel another course; the effect of knocking her up at two o'clock in the morning would hardly be to soothe her. He looked at six newspapers the next day and found in them never a good word for her. They were well enough about the piece, but they were unanimous as to the disappointment caused by the young actress whose former efforts had excited such hopes and on whom, on this occasion, such pressing responsibilities rested. They asked in chorus what was the matter with her, and they declared in chorus that the play, which was not without promise, was handicapped (they all used the same word) by the odd want of correspondence between the heroine and her interpreter. Wayworth drove early to Notting Hill, but he didn't take the newspapers with him; Violet Grey could be trusted to have sent out for them by the peep of dawn and to have fed her anguish full. She declined to see him—she only sent down word by her aunt that she was extremely unwell and should be unable to act that night unless she were suffered to spend the day unmolested and in bed. Wayworth sat for an hour with the old lady, who understood everything and to whom he could speak frankly. She gave him a touching picture of her niece's condition, which was all the more vivid for the simple words in which it was expressed: "She feels she isn't right, you know—she feels she isn't right!"

"Tell her it doesn't matter—it doesn't matter a straw!" said Wayworth.

"And she's so proud—you know how proud she is!" the old lady went on.

"Tell her I'm more than satisfied, that I accept her gratefully as she is."

"She says she injures your play, that she ruins it," said his interlocutress.

"She'll improve, immensely—she'll grow into the part," the young man continued.

"She'd improve if she knew how—but she says she doesn't. She has given all she has got, and she doesn't know what's wanted."

"What's wanted is simply that she should go straight on and trust me."

"How can she trust you when she feels she's losing you?"

"Losing me?" Wayworth cried.

"You'll never forgive her if your play is taken off!"

"It will run six months," said the author of the piece.

The old lady laid her hand on his arm. "What will you do for her if it does?"

He looked at Violet Grey's aunt a moment. "Do you say your niece is very proud?"

"Too proud for her dreadful profession."

"Then she wouldn't wish you to ask me that," Wayworth answered, getting up.

When he reached home he was very tired, and for a person to whom it was open to consider that he had scored a success he spent a remarkably dismal day. All his restlessness had gone, and fatigue and depression possessed him. He sank into his old chair by the fire and sat there for hours with his eyes closed. His landlady came in to bring his luncheon and mend the fire, but he feigned to be asleep, so as not to be spoken to. It is to be supposed that sleep at last overtook him, for about the hour that dusk began to gather he had an extraordinary impression, a visit that, it would seem, could have belonged to no waking consciousness. Nona Vincent, in face and form, the living heroine of his play, rose before him in his little silent room, sat down with him at his dingy fireside. She was not Violet Grey, she was not Mrs. Alsager, she was not any woman he had seen upon earth, nor was it any masquerade of friendship or of penitence. Yet she was more familiar to him than the women he had known best, and she was ineffably beautiful and consoling. She filled the poor room with her presence, the effect of which was as soothing as some odor of incense. She was as quiet as an affectionate sister, and there was no surprise in her being there. Nothing more real had ever befallen him, and nothing, somehow, more reassuring. He felt her hand rest upon his own, and all his senses seemed to open to her message. She struck him, in the strangest way, both as his creation and as his inspirer, and she gave him the happiest consciousness of success. If she was so charming, in the red firelight, in her vague, clear-colored garments, it was because he had made her so, and yet if the weight seemed lifted from his spirit it was because she drew it away. When she bent her deep eyes upon him they seemed to speak of safety and freedom and to make a green garden of the future. From time to time she smiled and said: "I live—I live—I live." How long she stayed he couldn't have told, but when his landlady blundered in with the lamp Nona Vincent was no longer there. He rubbed his eyes, but no dream had ever been so intense; and as he slowly got out of his chair it was with a deep still joy—the joy of the artist—in the thought of how right he had been, how exactly like herself he had made her. She had come to show him that. At the end of five minutes, however, he felt sufficiently mystified to call his landlady back—he wanted to ask her a question. When the good woman reappeared the question hung fire an instant; then it shaped itself as the inquiry:

"Has any lady been here?"

"No, sir—no lady at all."

The woman seemed slightly scandalized. "Not Miss Vincent?"

"Miss Vincent, sir?"

"The young lady of my play, don't you know?"

"Oh, sir, you mean Miss Violet Grey!"

"No I don't, at all. I think I mean Mrs. Alsager."

"There has been no Mrs. Alsager, sir."

"Nor anybody at all like her?"

The woman looked at him as if she wondered what had suddenly taken him. Then she asked in an injured tone: "Why shouldn't I have told you if you'd 'ad callers, sir?"

"I thought you might have thought I was asleep."

"Indeed you were, sir, when I came in with the lamp—and well you'd earned it, Mr. Wayworth!"

The landlady came back an hour later to bring him a telegram; it was just as he had begun to dress to dine at his club and go down to the theatre.

"See me tonight in front, and don't come near me till it's over."

It was in these words that Violet communicated her wishes for the evening. He obeyed them to the letter; he watched her from the depths of a box. He was in no position to say how she might have struck him the night before, but what he saw during these charmed hours filled him with admiration and gratitude. She *was* in it, this time; she had pulled herself together, she had taken possession, she was felicitous at every turn. Fresh from his revelation of Nona he was in a position to judge, and as he judged he exulted. He was thrilled and carried away, and he was moreover intensely curious to know what had happened to her, by what unfathomable art she had managed in a few hours to effect such a change of base. It was as if *she* had had a revelation of Nona, so convincing a clearness had been breathed upon the picture. He kept himself quiet in the *entr'actes*—he would speak to her only at the end; but before the play was half over the manager burst into his box.

"It's prodigious, what she's up to!" cried Mr. Loder, almost more bewildered than gratified. "She has gone in for a new reading—a blessed somersault in the air!"

"Is it quite different?" Wayworth asked, sharing his mystification.

"Different? Hyperion to a satyr! It's devilish good, my boy!"

"It's devilish good," said Wayworth, "and it's in a different key altogether from the key of her rehearsal."

"I'll run you six months!" the manager declared; and he rushed round again to the actress, leaving Wayworth with a sense that she had already pulled him through. She had with the audience an immense personal success.

When he went behind, at the end, he had to wait for her; she only showed herself when she was ready to leave the theatre. Her aunt had been in her dressing-room with her, and the two ladies appeared together. The girl passed him quickly, motioning him to say nothing till they should have got out of the place. He saw that she was immensely excited, lifted altogether above her common artistic level. The old lady said to him: "You must come home to supper with us: it has been all arranged." They had a brougham, with a little third seat, and he got into it with them. It was a long time before the actress would speak. She leaned back in her corner, giving no sign but still heaving a little, like a subsiding sea, and with all her triumph in the eyes that shone through the darkness. The old lady was hushed to awe, or at least to discretion, and Wayworth was happy enough to wait. He had really to wait till they had alighted at Notting Hill, where the elder of his companions went to see that supper had been attended to.

"I was better—I was better," said Violet Grey, throwing off her cloak in the little drawing-room.

"You were perfection. You'll be like that every night, won't you?"

She smiled at him. "Every night? There can scarcely be a miracle every day."

"What do you mean by a miracle?"

"I've had a revelation."

Wayward stared. "At what hour?"

"The right hour—this afternoon. Just in time to save me—and to save *you*."

"At five o'clock? Do you mean you had a visit?"

"She came to me—she stayed two hours."

"Two hours? Nona Vincent?"

"Mrs. Alsager." Violet Grey smiled more deeply. "It's the same thing."

"And how did Mrs. Alsager save you?"

"By letting me look at her. By letting me hear her speak. By letting me know her."

"And what did she say to you?"

"Kind things—encouraging, intelligent things."

"Ah, the dear woman!" Wayworth cried.

"You ought to like her—she likes *you*. She was just what I wanted," the actress added.

"Do you mean she talked to you about Nona?"

"She said you thought she was like her. She *is*—she's exquisite."

"She's exquisite," Wayworth repeated. "Do you mean she tried to coach you?"

"Oh, no—she only said she would be so glad if it would help me to see her. And I felt it did help me. I don't know what took place—she only sat there, and she held my hand and smiled at me, and she had tact and grace, and she had goodness and beauty, and she soothed my nerves and lighted up my imagination. Somehow she seemed to *give* it all to me. I took it—I took it. I kept her before me, I drank her in. For the first time, in the whole study of the part, I had my model—I could make my copy. All my courage came back to me, and other things came that I hadn't felt before. She was different—she was delightful; as I've said, she was a revelation. She kissed me when she went away—and you may guess if I kissed *her*. We were awfully affectionate, but it's *you* she likes!" said Violet Grey.

Wayworth had never been more interested in his life, and he had rarely been more mystified. "Did she wear vague, clear-colored garments?" he asked, after a moment.

Violet Grey stared, laughed, then bade him go in to supper. "*You* know how she dresses!"

He was very well pleased at supper, but he was silent and a little solemn. He said he would go to see Mrs. Alsager the next day. He did so, but he was told at her door that she had returned to Torquay. She remained there all winter, all spring, and the next time he saw her his play had run two hundred nights and he had married Violet Grey. His plays sometimes succeed, but his wife is not in them now, nor in any others. At these representations Mrs. Alsager continues frequently to be present.

THE REAL THING

I

When the porter's wife (she used to answer the house-bell), announced "A gentleman—with a lady, sir," I had, as I often had in those days, for the wish was father to the thought, an immediate vision of sitters. Sitters my visitors in this case proved to be; but not in the sense I should have preferred. However, there was nothing at first to indicate that they might not have come for a portrait. The gentleman, a man of fifty, very high and very straight, with a moustache slightly grizzled and a dark gray walking-coat admirably fitted, both of which I noted professionally—I don't mean as a barber or yet as a tailor—would have struck me as a celebrity if celebrities often were striking. It was a truth of which I had for some time been conscious that a figure with a good deal of frontage was, as one might say, almost never a public institution. A glance at the lady helped to remind me of this paradoxical law: she also looked too distinguished to be a "personality." Moreover one would scarcely come across two variations together.

Neither of the pair spoke immediately—they only prolonged the preliminary gaze which suggested that each wished to give the other a chance. They were visibly shy; they stood there letting me take them in—which, as I afterwards perceived, was the most practical thing they could have done. In this way their embarrassment served their cause. I had seen people painfully reluctant to mention that they desired anything so gross as to be represented on canvas; but the scruples of my new friends appeared almost insurmountable. Yet the gentleman might have said "I should like a portrait of my wife," and the lady might have said "I should like a portrait of my husband." Perhaps they were not husband and wife—this naturally would make the matter more delicate. Perhaps they wished to be done together— in which case they ought to have brought a third person to break the news.

"We come from Mr. Rivet," the lady said at last, with a dim smile which had the effect of a moist sponge passed over a "sunk" piece of painting, as well as of a vague allusion to vanished beauty. She was as tall and straight, in her degree, as her companion, and with ten years less to carry. She looked as sad as a woman could look whose face was not charged with expression; that is her tinted oval mask showed friction as an exposed surface shows it. The hand of time had played over her freely, but only to simplify. She was slim and stiff, and so well-dressed, in dark blue cloth, with lappets and pockets and buttons, that it was clear she employed the same tailor as her husband. The couple had an indefinable air of prosperous thrift—they evidently got a good deal of luxury for their money. If I was to be one of their luxuries it would behoove me to consider my terms.

"Ah, Claude Rivet recommended me?" I inquired; and I added that it was very kind of him, though I could reflect that, as he only painted landscape, this was not a sacrifice.

The lady looked very hard at the gentleman, and the gentleman looked round the room. Then staring at the floor a moment and stroking his moustache, he rested his pleasant eyes on me with the remark:

"He said you were the right one."

"I try to be, when people want to sit."

"Yes, we should like to," said the lady anxiously.

"Do you mean together?"

My visitors exchanged a glance. "If you could do anything

with *me*, I suppose it would be double," the gentleman stammered.

"Oh yes, there's naturally a higher charge for two figures than for one."

"We should like to make it pay," the husband confessed.

"That's very good of you," I returned, appreciating so unwonted a sympathy—for I supposed he meant pay the artist.

A sense of strangeness seemed to dawn on the lady. "We mean for the illustrations—Mr. Rivet said you might put one in."

"Put one in—an illustration?" I was equally confused.

"Sketch her off, you know," said the gentleman, coloring.

It was only then that I understood the service Claude Rivet had rendered me; he had told them that I worked in black and white, for magazines, for story-books, for sketches of contemporary life, and consequently had frequent employment for models. These things were true, but it was not less true (I may confess it now—whether because the aspiration was to lead to everything or to nothing I leave the reader to guess), that I couldn't get the honors, to say nothing of the emoluments, of a great painter of portraits out of my head. My "illustrations" were my pot-boilers; I looked to a different branch of art (far and away the most interesting it had always seemed to me), to perpetuate my fame. There was no shame in looking to it also to make my fortune; but that fortune was by so much further from being made from the moment my visitors wished to be "done" for nothing. I was disappointed; for in the pictorial sense I had immediately *seen* them. I had seized their type—I had already settled what I would do with it. Something that wouldn't absolutely have pleased them, I afterwards reflected.

"Ah, you're—you're—a—?" I began, as soon as I had mastered my surprise. I couldn't bring out the dingy word "models"; it seemed to fit the case so little.

"We haven't had much practice," said the lady.

"We've got to *do* something, and we've thought that an artist in your line might perhaps make something of us," her husband threw off. He further mentioned that they didn't know many artists and that they had gone first, on the off-chance (he painted views of course, but sometimes put in figures—perhaps I remembered), to Mr. Rivet, whom they had met a few years before at a place in Norfolk where he was sketching.

"We used to sketch a little ourselves," the lady hinted.

"It's very awkward, but we absolutely *must* do something," her husband went on.

"Of course, we're not so *very* young," she admitted, with a wan smile.

With the remark that I might as well know something

more about them, the husband had handed me a card extracted from a neat new pocket-book (their appurtenances were all of the freshest) and inscribed with the words "Major Monarch." Impressive as these words were they didn't carry my knowledge much further; but my visitor presently added: "I've left the army, and we've had the misfortune to lose our money. In fact our means are dreadfully small."

"It's an awful bore," said Mrs. Monarch.

They evidently wished to be discreet—to take care not to swagger because they were gentlefolks. I perceived they would have been willing to recognize this as something of a drawback, at the same time that I guessed at an underlying sense—their consolation in adversity—that they *had* their points. They certainly had; but these advantages struck me as preponderantly social; such for instance as would help to make a drawing-room look well. However, a drawing-room was always, or ought to be, a picture.

In consequence of his wife's allusion to their age Major Monarch observed: "Naturally, it's more for the figure that we thought of going in. We can still hold ourselves up." On the instant I saw that the figure was indeed their strong point. His "naturally" didn't sound vain, but it lighted up the question. "*She* has got the best," he continued, nodding at his wife, with a pleasant after-dinner absence of circumlocution. I could only reply, as if we were in fact sitting over our wine, that this didn't prevent his own from being very good; which led him in turn to rejoin: "We thought that if you ever have to do people like us, we might be something like it. *She*, particularly—for a lady in a book, you know."

I was so amused by them that, to get more of it, I did my best to take their point of view; and though it was an embarrassment to find myself appraising physically, as if they were animals on hire, a pair whom I should have expected to meet only in one of the relations in which criticism is tacit, I looked at Mrs. Monarch judicially enough to be able to exclaim, after a moment, with conviction: "Oh yes, a lady in a book!" She was singularly like a bad illustration.

"We'll stand up, if you like," said the Major; and he raised himself before me with a really grand air.

I could take his measure at a glance—he was six feet two and a perfect gentleman. It would have paid any club in process of formation and in want of a stamp to engage him at a salary to stand in the principal window. What struck me immediately was that in coming to me they had rather missed their vocation; they could surely have been turned to better account for advertising purposes. I couldn't of course see the thing in detail, but I could see them make someone's fortune—I don't mean their own. There was something in them for a waistcoat-maker, an hotel-keeper or a soap-vendor. I could imagine "We always use it" pinned on their bosoms with the greatest effect; I had a vision of the promptitude with which they would launch a table d'hôte.

Mrs. Monarch sat still, not from pride but from shyness, and presently her husband said to her: "Get up my dear and show how smart you are." She obeyed, but she had no need to get up to show it. She walked to the end of the studio, and then she came back blushing, with her fluttered eyes on her husband. I was reminded of an incident I had accidentally had a glimpse of in Paris—being with a friend there, a dramatist about to produce a play—when an actress came to him to ask to be entrusted with a part. She went through her paces before him, walked up and down as Mrs. Monarch was doing. Mrs. Monarch did it quite as well, but I abstained from applauding. It was very odd to see such people apply for such poor pay. She looked as if she had ten thousand a year. Her husband had used the word that described her: she was, in the London current jargon, essentially and typically "smart." Her figure was, in the same order of ideas, conspicuously and irreproachably "good." For a woman of her age her waist was surprisingly small; her elbow moreover had the orthodox crook. She held her head at the conventional angle; but why did she come to *me?* She ought to have tried on jackets at a big shop. I feared my visitors were not only destitute, but "artistic"—which would be a great complication. When she sat down again I thanked her, observing that what a draughtsman most valued in his model was the faculty of keeping quiet.

"Oh, *she* can keep quiet," said Major Monarch. Then he added, jocosely: "I've always kept her quiet."

"I'm not a nasty fidget, am I?" Mrs. Monarch appealed to her husband.

He addressed his answer to me. "Perhaps it isn't out of place to mention—because we ought to be quite business-like, oughtn't we?—that when I married her she was known as the Beautiful Statue."

"Oh dear!" said Mrs. Monarch, ruefully.

"Of course I should want a certain amount of expression," I rejoined.

"Of *course!*" they both exclaimed.

"And then I suppose you know that you'll get awfully tired."

"Oh, we *never* get tired!" they eagerly cried.

"Have you had any kind of practice?"

They hesitated—they looked at each other. "We've been photographed, *immensely,*" said Mrs. Monarch.

"She means the fellows have asked us," added the Major.

"I see—because you're so good-looking."

"I don't know what they thought, but they were always after us."

"We always got our photographs for nothing," smiled Mrs. Monarch.

"We might have brought some, my dear," her husband remarked.

"I'm not sure we have any left. We've given quantities away," she explained to me.

"With our autographs and that sort of thing," said the Major.

"Are they to be got in the shops?" I inquired, as a harmless pleasantry.

"Oh, yes; hers—they used to be."

"Not now," said Mrs. Monarch, with her eyes on the floor.

II

I could fancy the "sort of thing" they put on the presentation-copies of their photographs, and I was sure they wrote a beautiful hand. It was odd how quickly I was sure of everything that concerned them. If they were now so poor as to have to earn shillings and pence, they never had had much of a margin. Their good looks had been their capital, and they had good-humoredly made the most of the career that this resource marked out for them. It was in their faces, the blankness, the deep intellectual repose of the twenty years of country-house visiting which had given them pleasant intonations. I could see the sunny drawing-rooms, sprinkled with periodicals she didn't read, in which Mrs. Monarch had continuously sat; I could see the wet shrubberies in which she had walked, equipped to admiration for either exercise. I could see the rich covers the Major had helped to shoot and the wonderful garments in which, late at night, he repaired to the smoking-room to talk about them. I could imagine their leggings and waterproofs, their knowing tweeds and rugs, their rolls of sticks and cases of tackle and neat umbrellas; and I could evoke the exact appearance of their servants and the compact variety of their luggage on the platforms of country stations.

They gave small tips, but they were liked; they didn't do anything themselves, but they were welcome. They looked so well everywhere; they gratified the general relish for stature, complexion and "form." They knew it without fatuity or vulgarity, and they respected themselves in consequence. They were not superficial; they were thorough and kept themselves up—it had been their line. People with such a taste for activity had to have some line. I could feel how, even in a dull house, they could have been counted upon for cheerfulness. At present something had happened—it didn't matter what, their little income had grown less, it had grown least—and they had to do something for pocket-money. Their friends liked them, but didn't like to support them. There was something about them that represented credit—their clothes, their manners, their type; but if credit is a large empty pocket in which an occasional chink reverberates, the chink at least must be audible. What they wanted of me was to help to make it so. Fortunately they had no children—I soon divined that. They would also perhaps wish our relations to be kept secret: this was why it was "for the figure"—the reproduction of the face would betray them.

I liked them—they were so simple; and I had no objection to them if they would suit. But, somehow, with all their perfections I didn't easily believe in them. After all they were amateurs, and the ruling passion of my life was the detestation of the amateur. Combined with this was another perversity—an innate preference for the represented subject over the real one: the defect of the real one was so apt to be a lack of representation. I liked things that appeared; then one was sure. Whether they *were* or not was a subordinate and almost always a profitless question. There were other considerations, the first of which was that I already had two or three people in use, notably a young person with big feet, in alpaca, from Kilburn, who for a couple of years had come to me regularly for my illustrations and with whom I was still— perhaps ignobly—satisfied. I frankly explained to my visitors how the case stood; but they had taken more precautions than I supposed. They had reasoned out their opportunity, for Claude Rivet had told them of the projected *édition de luxe* of one of the writers of our day—the rarest of the novelists—who, long neglected by the multitudinous vulgar and dearly prized by the attentive (need I mention Philip Vincent?) had had the happy fortune of seeing, late in life, the dawn and then the full light of a higher criticism—an estimate in which, on the part of the public, there was something really of expiation. The edition in question, planned by a publisher of taste, was practically an act of high reparation; the wood-cuts with which it was to be enriched were the homage of English art to one of the most independent representatives of English letters. Major and Mrs. Monarch confessed to me that they had hoped I might be able to work *them* into my share of the enterprise. They knew I was to do the first of the books, "Rutland Ramsay," but I had to make clear to them that my participation in the rest of the affair—this first book was to be a test—was to depend on the satisfaction I should give. If this should be limited my employers would drop me without a scruple. It was therefore a crisis for me, and naturally I was making special preparations, looking about for new people, if they should be necessary, and securing the best types. I admitted however that I should like to settle down to two or three good models who would do for everything.

"Should we have often to—a—put on special clothes?" Mrs. Monarch timidly demanded.

"Dear, yes—that's half the business."

"And should we be expected to supply our own costumes?"

"Oh, no; I've got a lot of things. A painter's models put on—or put off—anything he likes."

"And do you mean—a—the same?"

"The same?"

Mrs. Monarch looked at her husband again.

"Oh, she was just wondering," he explained, "if the costumes are in *general* use." I had to confess that they were, and I mentioned further that some of them (I had a lot of genuine, greasy last-century things), had served their time, a hundred years ago, on living, world-stained men and women. "We'll put on anything that fits," said the Major.

"Oh, I arrange that—they fit in the pictures."

"I'm afraid I should do better for the modern books. I would come as you like," said Mrs. Monarch.

"She has got a lot of clothes at home: they might do for contemporary life," her husband continued.

"Oh, I can fancy scenes in which you'd be quite natural." And indeed I could see the slipshod rearrangements of stale properties—the stories I tried to produce pictures for without the exasperation of reading them—whose sandy tracts the good lady might help to people. But I had to return to the fact that for this sort of work—the daily mechanical grind—I was already equipped; the people I was working with were fully adequate.

"We only thought we might be more like *some* characters," said Mrs. Monarch mildly, getting up.

Her husband also rose; he stood looking at me with a dim wistfulness that was touching in so fine a man. "Wouldn't it be rather a pull sometimes to have—a—to have—?" He hung fire; he wanted me to help him by phrasing what he meant. But I couldn't—I didn't know. So he brought it out, awkwardly: "The *real* thing; a gentleman, you know, or a lady." I was quite ready to give a general assent—I admitted that there was a great deal in that. This encouraged Major Monarch to say, following up his appeal with an unacted gulp: "It's awfully hard—we've tried everything." The gulp was communicative; it proved too much for his wife. Before I knew it Mrs. Monarch had dropped again upon a divan and burst into tears. Her husband sat down beside her, holding one of her hands; whereupon she quickly dried her eyes with the other, while I felt embarrassed as she looked up at me. "There isn't a confounded job I haven't applied for—waited for—prayed for. You can fancy we'd be pretty bad first. Secretaryships and that sort of thing? You might as well ask for a peerage. I'd be *anything*—I'm strong; a messenger or a coalheaver. I'd put on a gold-laced cap and open carriage-doors in front of the haberdasher's; I'd hang about a station, to carry portmanteaus; I'd be a postman. But they won't *look* at you; there are thousands, as good as yourself, already on the ground. *Gentlemen*, poor beggars, who have drunk their wine, who have kept their hunters!"

I was as reassuring as I knew how to be, and my visitors were presently on their feet again while, for the experiment, we agreed on an hour. We were discussing it when the door opened and Miss Churm came in with a wet umbrella. Miss Churm had to take the omnibus to Maida Vale and then walk half-a-mile. She looked a trifle blowsy and slightly splashed. I scarcely ever saw her come in without thinking afresh how odd it was that, being so little in herself, she should yet be so much in others. She was a meager little Miss Churm, but she was an ample heroine of romance. She was only a freckled cockney, but she could represent everything, from a fine lady to a shepherdess; she had the faculty, as she might have had a fine voice or long hair.

She couldn't spell, and she loved beer, but she had two or three "points," and practice, and a knack, and mother-wit, and a kind of whimsical sensibility, and a love of the theatre, and seven sisters, and not an ounce of respect, especially for the *h*. The first thing my visitors saw was that her umbrella was wet, and in their spotless perfection they visibly winced at it. The rain had come on since their arrival.

"I'm all in a soak; there *was* a mess of people in the 'bus. I wish you lived near a stytion," said Miss Churm. I requested her to get ready as quickly as possible, and she passed into the room in which she always changed her dress. But before going out she asked me what she was to get into this time.

"It's the Russian princess, don't you know?" I answered; "the one with the 'golden eyes,' in black velvet, for the long thing in the *Cheapside*."

"Golden eyes? I *say*!" cried Miss Churm, while my companions watched her with intensity as she withdrew. She always arranged herself, when she was late, before I could turn round; and I kept my visitors a little, on purpose, so that they might get an idea, from seeing her, what would be expected of themselves. I mentioned that she was quite my notion of an excellent model—she was really very clever.

"Do you think she looks like a Russian princess?" Major Monarch asked, with lurking alarm.

"When I make her, yes."

"Oh, if you have to *make* her—!" he reasoned, acutely.

"That's the most you can ask. There are so many that are not makeable."

"Well now, *here's* a lady"—and with a persuasive smile he passed his arm into his wife's—"who's already made!"

"Oh, I'm not a Russian princess," Mrs. Monarch protested, a little coldly. I could see that she had known some and didn't like them. There, immediately, was a complication of a kind that I never had to fear with Miss Churm.

This young lady came back in black velvet—the gown was rather rusty and very low on her lean shoulders—and with a Japanese fan in her red hands. I reminded her that in the scene I was doing she had to look over someone's head. "I forget whose it is; but it doesn't matter. Just look over a head."

"I'd rather look over a stove," said Miss Churm; and she took her station near the fire. She fell into position, settled herself into a tall attitude, gave a certain backward inclination to her head and a certain forward droop to her fan, and looked, at least to my prejudiced sense, distinguished and charming, foreign and dangerous. We left her looking so, while I went down-stairs with Major and Mrs. Monarch.

"I think I could come about as near it as that," said Mrs. Monarch.

"Oh, you think she's shabby, but you must allow for the alchemy of art."

However, they went off with an evident increase of comfort, founded on their demonstrable advantage in being the real thing. I could fancy them shuddering over Miss Churm. She was very droll about them when I went back, for I told her what they wanted.

"Well, if *she* can sit I'll tyke to bookkeeping," said my model.

"She's very lady-like," I replied, as an innocent form of aggravation.

"So much the worse for *you*. That means she can't turn round."

"She'll do for the fashionable novels."

"Oh yes, she'll *do* for them!" my model humorously declared. "Ain't they had enough without her?" I had often sociably denounced them to Miss Churm.

III

It was for the elucidation of a mystery in one of these works that I first tried Mrs. Monarch. Her husband came with her, to be useful if necessary—it was sufficiently clear that as a general thing he would prefer to come with her. At first I wondered if this were for "propriety's" sake—if he were going to be jealous and meddling. The idea was too tiresome, and if it had been confirmed it would speedily have brought our acquaintance to a close. But I soon saw there was nothing in it and that if he accompanied Mrs. Monarch it was (in addition to the chance of being wanted), simply because he had nothing else to do. When she was away from him his occupation was gone—she never *had* been away from him. I judged, rightly, that in their awkward situation their close union was their main comfort and that this union had no weak spot. It was a real marriage, an encouragement to the hesitating, a nut for pessimists to crack. Their address was humble (I remember afterwards thinking it had been the only thing about them that was really professional), and I could fancy the lamentable lodgings in which the Major would have been left alone. He could bear them with his wife—he couldn't bear them without her.

He had too much tact to try and make himself agreeable when he couldn't be useful; so he simply sat and waited, when I was too absorbed in my work to talk. But I liked to make him talk—it made my work, when it didn't interrupt it, less sordid, less special. To listen to him was to combine the excitement of going out with the economy of staying at home. There was only one hindrance: that I seemed not to know any of the people he and his wife had known. I think he wondered extremely, during the term of our intercourse, whom the deuce I *did* know. He hadn't a stray sixpence of an idea to fumble for; so we didn't spin it very fine—we confined ourselves to questions of leather and even of liquor (saddlers and breeches-makers and how to get good claret cheap), and matters like "good trains" and the habits of small game. His lore on these last subjects was astonishing, he managed to interweave the station-master with the ornithologist. When he couldn't talk about greater things he could talk cheerfully about smaller, and since I couldn't accompany him into reminiscences of the fashionable world he could lower the conversation without a visible effort to my level.

So earnest a desire to please was touching in a man who could so easily have knocked one down. He looked after the fire and had an opinion on the draught of the stove, without my asking him, and I could see that he thought many of my arrangements not half clever enough. I remember telling him that if I were only rich I would offer him a salary to come and teach me how to live. Sometimes he gave a random sigh, of which the essence was: "Give me even such a bare old barrack as *this*, and I'd do something with it!" When I wanted to use him he came alone; which was an illustration of the superior courage of women. His wife could bear her solitary second floor, and she was in general more discreet; showing by various small reserves that she was alive to the propriety of keeping our relations markedly professional—not letting them slide into sociability. She wished it to remain clear that she and the Major were employed, not cultivated, and if she approved of me as a superior, who could be kept in his place, she never thought me quite good enough for an equal.

She sat with great intensity, giving the whole of her mind to it, and was capable of remaining for an hour almost as motionless as if she were before a photographer's lens. I could see she had been photographed often, but somehow the very habit that made her good for that purpose unfitted her for mine. At first I was extremely pleased with her lady-like air, and it was a satisfaction, on coming to follow her lines, to see how good they were and how far they could lead the pencil. But after a few times I began to find her too insurmountably stiff; do what I would with it my drawing looked like a photograph or a copy of a photograph. Her figure had no variety of expression—she herself had no sense of variety. You may say that this was my business, was only a question of placing her. I placed her in every conceivable position, but she managed to obliterate their differences. She was always a lady certainly, and into the bargain was always the same lady. She was the real thing, but always the same thing. There were moments when I was oppressed by the serenity of her confidence that she *was* the real thing. All her dealings with me and all her husband's were an implication that this was lucky for *me*. Meanwhile I found myself trying to invent types that approached her own, instead of making her own transform itself—in the clever way that was not impossible, for instance, to poor Miss Churm. Arrange as I would and take the precautions I would, she always, in my pictures, came out too tall—landing me in the dilemma of having represented a fascinating woman as seven feet high, which, out of respect perhaps to my own very much scantier inches, was far from my idea of such a personage.

The case was worse with the Major—nothing I could do would keep *him* down, so that he became useful only for the representation of brawny giants. I adored variety and range, I cherished human accidents, the illustrative note; I wanted to characterize closely, and the thing in the world I most hated was the danger of being ridden by a type. I had quarreled with some of my friends about it—I had parted company with them for maintaining that one *had* to be, and that if the type was beautiful (witness Raphael and Leonardo), the servitude was only a gain. I was neither Leonardo nor Raphael; I might only be a presumptuous young modern searcher, but I held that everything was to be sacrificed sooner than character. When they averred that the haunting type in question could easily *be* character, I retorted, perhaps superficially: "Whose?" It couldn't be everybody's—it might end in being nobody's.

After I had drawn Mrs. Monarch a dozen times I perceived more clearly than before that the value of such a model as Miss Churm resided precisely in the fact that she had no positive stamp, combined of course with the other fact that what she did have was a curious and inexplicable talent for imitation. Her usual appearance was like a curtain which she could draw up at request for a capital performance. This performance was simply suggestive; but it was a word to the wise—it was vivid and pretty. Sometimes, even, I thought it, though she was plain herself, too insipidly pretty; I made it a reproach to her that the figures drawn from her were monotonously (*bêtement*, as we used to say) graceful. Nothing made her more angry: it was so much her pride to feel that she could sit for characters that had nothing in common with each other. She would accuse me at such moments of taking away her "reputytion."

It suffered a certain shrinkage, this queer quantity, from the repeated visits of my new friends. Miss Churm was greatly in demand, never in want of employment, so I had no scruple in putting her off occasionally, to try them more at my ease. It was certainly amusing at first to do the real thing—it was amusing to do Major Monarch's trousers. They *were* the real thing, even if he did come out colossal. It was amusing to do his wife's back hair (it was so mathematically neat), and the particular "smart" tension of her tight stays. She lent herself especially to positions in which the face was somewhat averted or blurred; she abounded in lady-like back views and *profils perdus*. When she stood erect she took naturally one of the attitudes in which court-painters represent queens and princesses; so that I found myself wondering whether, to draw out this accomplishment, I couldn't get the editor of the *Cheapside* to publish a really royal romance, "A Tale of Buckingham Palace." Sometimes, however, the real thing and the make-believe came into contact; by which I mean that Miss Churm, keeping an appointment or coming to make one on days when I had much work in hand, encountered her invidious rivals. The encounter was not on their part, for they noticed her no more than if she had been the housemaid; not from intentional loftiness, but simply because, as yet, professionally, they didn't know how to fraternize, as I could guess that they would have liked—or at least that the Major would. They couldn't talk about the omnibus—they always walked; and they didn't know what else to try—she wasn't interested in good trains or cheap claret. Besides, they must have felt—in the air—that she was amused at them, secretly derisive of their ever knowing how. She was not a person to conceal her skepticism if she had had a chance to show it. On the other hand Mrs. Monarch didn't think her tidy; for why else did she take pains to say to me (it was going out of the way, for Mrs. Monarch), that she didn't like dirty women?

One day when my young lady happened to be present with my other sitters (she even dropped in, when it was convenient, for a chat), I asked her to be so good as to lend a hand in getting tea—a service with which she was familiar and which was one of a class that, living as I did in a small way, with slender domestic resources, I often appealed to my models to render. They liked to lay hands on my property, to break the sitting, and sometimes the china—I made them feel Bohemian. The next time I saw Miss Churm after this incident she surprised me greatly by making a scene about it—she accused me of having wished to humiliate her. She had not resented the outrage at the time, but had seemed obliging and amused, enjoying the comedy of asking Mrs. Monarch, who sat vague and silent, whether she would have cream and sugar, and putting an exaggerated simper into the question. She had tried intonations—as if she too wished to pass for the real thing; till I was afraid my other visitors would take offense.

Oh, *they* were determined not to do this; and their touching patience was the measure of their great need. They would sit by the hour, uncomplaining, till I was ready to use them; they would come back on the chance of being wanted and would walk away cheerfully if they were not. I used to go to the door with them to see in what magnificent order they retreated. I tried to find other employment for them—I introduced them to several artists. But they didn't "take," for reasons I could appreciate, and I became conscious, rather anxiously, that after such disappointments they fell back upon me with a heavier weight. They did me the honor to think that it was I who was most *their* form. They were not picturesque enough for the painters, and in those days there were not so many serious workers in black and white. Besides, they had an eye to the great job I had mentioned to them—

they had secretly set their hearts on supplying the right essence for my pictorial vindication of our fine novelist. They knew that for this undertaking I should want no costume-effects, none of the frippery of past ages—that it was a case in which everything would be contemporary and satirical and, presumably, genteel. If I could work them into it their future would be assured, for the labor would of course be long and the occupation steady.

One day Mrs. Monarch came without her husband—she explained his absence by his having had to go to the City. While she sat there in her usual anxious stiffness there came, at the door, a knock which I immediately recognized as the subdued appeal of a model out of work. It was followed by the entrance of a young man whom I easily perceived to be a foreigner and who proved in fact an Italian acquainted with no English word but my name, which he uttered in a way that made it seem to include all others. I had not then visited his country, nor was I proficient in his tongue; but as he was not so meanly constituted—what Italian is?—as to depend only on that member for expression he conveyed to me, in famil-iar but graceful mimicry, that he was in search of exactly the employment in which the lady before me was engaged. I was not struck with him at first, and while I continued to draw I emitted rough sounds of discouragement and dismissal. He stood his ground, however, not importunately, but with

a dumb, dog-like fidelity in his eyes which amounted to innocent impudence—the manner of a devoted servant (he might
have been in the house for years), unjustly suspected. Suddenly I saw that this very attitude and expression made a picture, whereupon I told him to sit down and wait till I should
be free. There was another picture in the way he obeyed me,
and I observed as I worked that there were others still in the
way he looked wonderingly, with his head thrown back, about
the high studio. He might have been crossing himself in St.
Peter's. Before I finished I said to myself: "The fellow's a bank-
rupt orange-monger, but he's a treasure."

When Mrs. Monarch withdrew he passed across the room
like a flash to open the door for her, standing there with the
rapt, pure gaze of the young Dante spellbound by the young
Beatrice. As I never insisted, in such situations, on the blankness of the British domestic, I reflected that he had the making of a servant (and I needed one, but couldn't pay him to
be only that), as well as of a model; in short I made up my
mind to adopt my bright adventurer if he would agree to offi-
ciate in the double capacity. He jumped at my offer, and in the
event my rashness (for I had known nothing about him), was
not brought home to me. He proved a sympathetic though a
desultory ministrant, and had in a wonderful degree the *sen-
timent de la pose*. It was uncultivated, instinctive; a part of the
happy instinct which had guided him to my door and helped

him to spell out my name on the card nailed to it. He had had no other introduction to me than a guess, from the shape of my high north window, seen outside, that my place was a studio and that as a studio it would contain an artist. He had wandered to England in search of fortune, like other itinerants, and had embarked, with a partner and a small green handcart, on the sale of penny ices. The ices had melted away and the partner had dissolved in their train. My young man wore tight yellow trousers with reddish stripes and his name was Oronte. He was sallow but fair, and when I put him into some old clothes of my own he looked like an Englishman. He was as good as Miss Churm, who could look, when required, like an Italian.

IV

I thought Mrs. Monarch's face slightly convulsed when, on her coming back with her husband, she found Oronte installed. It was strange to have to recognize in a scrap of a lazzarone a competitor to her magnificent Major. It was she who scented danger first, for the Major was anecdotically unconscious. But Oronte gave us tea, with a hundred eager confusions (he had never seen such a queer process), and I think she thought better of me for having at last an "establishment." They saw a couple of drawings that I had made of the establishment, and Mrs. Monarch hinted that it never would have struck her that he had sat for them. "Now the drawings you make from *us*, they look exactly like us," she reminded me, smiling in triumph; and I recognized that this was indeed just their defect. When I drew the Monarchs I couldn't, somehow, get away from them—get into the character I wanted to represent; and I had not the least desire my model should be discoverable in my picture. Miss Churm never was, and Mrs. Monarch thought I hid her, very properly, because she was vulgar; whereas if she was lost it was only as the dead who go to heaven are lost—in the gain of an angel the more.

By this time I had got a certain start with "Rutland Ramsay," the first novel in the great projected series; that is I had produced a dozen drawings, several with the help of the Major and his wife, and I had sent them in for approval. My understanding with the publishers, as I have already hinted, had been that I was to be left to do my work, in this particular case, as I liked, with the whole book committed to me; but my connection with the rest of the series was only contingent. There were moments when, frankly, it *was* a comfort to have the real thing under one's hand; for there were characters in "Rutland Ramsay" that were very much like it. There were people presumably as straight as the Major and women of as good a fashion as Mrs. Monarch. There was a great deal of country-house life—treated, it is true, in a fine, fanciful, ironical, generalized way—and there was a considerable implication of knickerbockers and kilts. There were certain things I had to settle at the outset; such things for instance as the exact appearance of the hero, the particular bloom of the heroine. The author of course gave me a lead, but there was a margin for interpretation. I took the Monarchs into my confidence, I told them frankly what I was about, I mentioned my embarrassments and alternatives. "Oh, take *him!*" Mrs. Monarch murmured sweetly, looking at her husband; and "What could you want better than my wife?" the Major inquired, with the comfortable candor that now prevailed between us.

I was not obliged to answer these remarks—I was only obliged to place my sitters. I was not easy in mind, and I postponed, a little timidly perhaps, the solution of the question. The book was a large canvas, the other figures were numerous, and I worked off at first some of the episodes in which the hero and the heroine were not concerned. When once I had set *them* up I should have to stick to them—I couldn't make my young man seven feet high in one place and five feet nine in another. I inclined on the whole to the latter measurement, though the Major more than once reminded me that *he* looked about as young as anyone. It was indeed quite possible to arrange him, for the figure, so that it would have been difficult to detect his age. After the spontaneous Oronte had been with me a month, and after I had given him to understand several different times that his native exuberance would presently constitute an insurmountable barrier to our further intercourse, I waked to a sense of his heroic capacity. He was only five feet seven, but the remaining inches were latent. I tried him almost secretly at first, for I was really rather afraid of the judgment my other models would pass on such a choice. If they regarded Miss Churm as little better than a snare, what would they think of the representation by a person so little the real thing as an Italian street-vendor of a protagonist formed by a public school?

If I went a little in fear of them it was not because they bullied me, because they had got an oppressive foothold, but because in their really pathetic decorum and mysteriously permanent newness they counted on me so intensely. I was therefore very glad when Jack Hawley came home: he was always of such good counsel. He painted badly himself, but there was no one like him for putting his finger on the place. He had been absent from England for a year; he had been somewhere—I don't remember where—to get a fresh eye. I was in a good deal of dread of any such organ, but we were old friends; he had been away for months and a sense of emptiness was creeping into my life. I hadn't dodged a missile for a year.

He came back with a fresh eye, but with the same old black velvet blouse, and the first evening he spent in my studio we smoked cigarettes till the small hours. He had done no work himself, he had only got the eye; so the field was clear for the production of my little things. He wanted to see what I had done for the *Cheapside*, but he was disappointed in the exhibition. That at least seemed the meaning of two or three comprehensive groans which, as he lounged on my big divan, on a folded leg, looking at my latest drawings, issued from his lips with the smoke of the cigarette.

"What's the matter with you?" I asked.

"What's the matter with *you*?"

"Nothing save that I'm mystified."

"You are indeed. You're quite off the hinge. What's the meaning of this new fad?" And he tossed me, with visible irreverence, a drawing in which I happened to have depicted both my majestic models. I asked if he didn't think it good, and he replied that it struck him as execrable, given the sort of thing I had always represented myself to him as wishing to arrive at; but I let that pass, I was so anxious to see exactly what he meant. The two figures in the picture looked colossal, but I supposed this was *not* what he meant, inasmuch as, for aught he knew to the contrary, I might have been trying for that. I maintained that I was working exactly in the same way as when he last had done me the honor to commend me. "Well, there's a big hole somewhere," he answered; "wait a bit and I'll discover it." I depended upon him to do so: where else was the fresh eye? But he produced at last nothing more luminous than "I don't know—I don't like your types." This was lame, for a critic who had never consented to discuss with me anything but the question of execution, the direction of strokes and the mystery of values.

"In the drawings you've been looking at I think my types are very handsome."

"Oh, they won't do!"

"I've had a couple of new models."

"I see you have. *They* won't do."

"Are you very sure of that?"

"Absolutely—they're stupid."

"You mean *I* am—for I ought to get round that."

"You *can't*—with such people. Who are they?"

I told him, as far as was necessary, and he declared, heartlessly: "*Ce sont des gens qu'il faut mettre à la porte.*"

"You've never seen them; they're awfully good," I compassionately objected.

"Not seen them? Why, all this recent work of yours drops to pieces with them. It's all I want to see of them."

"No one else has said anything against it—the *Cheapside* people are pleased."

"Everyone else is an ass, and the *Cheapside* people the biggest asses of all. Come, don't pretend, at this time of day, to have pretty illusions about the public, especially about publishers and editors. It's not for *such* animals you work—

it's for those who know, *coloro che sanno*; so keep straight for *me* if you can't keep straight for yourself. There's a certain sort of thing you tried for from the first—and a very good thing it is. But this twaddle isn't *in it*." When I talked with Hawley later about "Rutland Ramsay" and its possible successors he declared that I must get back into my boat again or I would go to the bottom. His voice in short was the voice of warning.

I noted the warning, but I didn't turn my friends out of doors. They bored me a good deal; but the very fact that they bored me admonished me not to sacrifice them—if there was anything to be done with them—simply to irritation. As I look back at this phase they seem to me to have pervaded my life not a little. I have a vision of them as most of the time in my studio, seated, against the wall, on an old velvet bench to be out of the way, and looking like a pair of patient courtiers in a royal ante-chamber. I am convinced that during the coldest weeks of the winter they held their ground because it saved them fire. Their newness was losing its gloss, and it was impossible not to feel that they were objects of charity. Whenever Miss Churm arrived they went away, and after I was fairly launched in "Rutland Ramsay" Miss Churm arrived pretty often. They managed to express to me tacitly that they supposed I wanted her for the low life of the book, and I let them suppose it, since they had attempted to study the work—it was lying about the studio—without discovering that it dealt only with the highest circles. They had dipped into the most brilliant of our novelists without deciphering many passages. I still took an hour from them, now and again, in spite of Jack Hawley's warning: it would be time enough to dismiss them, if dismissal should be necessary, when the rigor of the season was over. Hawley had made their acquaintance—he had met them at my fireside—and thought them a ridiculous pair. Learning that he was a painter they tried to approach him, to show him too that they were the real thing; but he looked at them, across the big room, as if they were miles away: they were a compendium of everything that he most objected to in the social system of his country. Such people as that, all convention and patent-leather, with ejaculations that stopped conversation, had no business in a studio. A studio was a place to learn to see, and how could you see through a pair of feather beds?

The main inconvenience I suffered at their hands was that, at first, I was shy of letting them discover how my artful little servant had begun to sit to me for "Rutland Ramsay." They knew that I had been odd enough (they were prepared by this time to allow oddity to artists), to pick a foreign vagabond out of the streets, when I might have had a person with whiskers and credentials; but it was some time before they learned how high I rated his accomplishments. They found him in an attitude more than once, but they never doubted I was doing him as an organ-grinder. There were several things they never guessed, and one of them was that for a striking scene in the novel, in which a footman briefly figured, it occurred to me to make use of Major Monarch as the menial. I kept putting this off, I didn't like to ask him to don the livery—besides the difficulty of finding a livery to fit him. At last, one day late in the winter, when I was at work on the despised Oronte (he caught one's idea in an instant), and was in the glow of feeling that I was going very straight, they came in, the Major and his wife, with their society laugh about nothing (there was less and less to laugh at), like country-callers—they always reminded me of that—who have walked across the park after church and are presently persuaded to stay to luncheon. Luncheon was over, but they could stay to tea—I knew they wanted it. The fit was on me, however, and I couldn't let my ardor cool and my work wait, with the fading daylight, while my model prepared it. So I asked Mrs. Monarch if she would mind laying it out—a request which, for an instant, brought all the blood to her face. Her eyes were on her husband's for a second, and some mute telegraphy passed between them. Their folly was over the next instant; his cheerful shrewdness put an end to it. So far from pitying their wounded pride, I must add, I was moved to give it as complete a lesson as I could. They bustled about together and got out the cups and saucers and made the kettle boil. I know they felt as if they were waiting on my servant, and when the tea was prepared I said: "He'll have a cup, please—he's tired." Mrs. Monarch brought him one where he stood, and he took it from her as if he had been a gentleman at a party, squeezing a crush-hat with an elbow.

Then it came over me that she had made a great effort for me—made it with a kind of nobleness—and that I owed her a compensation. Each time I saw her after this I wondered what the compensation could be. I couldn't go on doing the wrong thing to oblige them. Oh, it *was* the wrong thing, the stamp of the work for which they sat—Hawley was not the only person to say it now. I sent in a large number of the drawings I had made for "Rutland Ramsay," and I received a warning that was more to the point than Hawley's. The artistic adviser of the house for which I was working was of opinion that many of my illustrations were not what had been looked for. Most of these illustrations were the subjects in which the Monarchs had figured. Without going into the question of what *had* been looked for, I saw at this rate I shouldn't get the other books to do. I hurled myself in despair upon Miss Churm, I put her through all her paces. I not only adopted Oronte publicly as my hero, but one morning when the Major looked in to see if I didn't require him to finish a figure for the *Cheapside*, for which he had begun to sit the week before, I told him that I had changed my mind—I would do the drawing from my man. At this my visitor turned pale and stood looking at me. "Is *he* your idea of an English gentleman?" he asked.

I was disappointed, I was nervous, I wanted to get on with my work; so I replied with irritation: "Oh, my dear Major—I can't be ruined for *you!*"

He stood another moment; then, without a word, he quitted the studio. I drew a long breath when he was gone, for I said to myself that I shouldn't see him again. I had not told him definitely that I was in danger of having my work rejected, but I was vexed at his not having felt the catastrophe in the air, read with me the moral of our fruitless collaboration, the lesson that, in the deceptive atmosphere of art, even the highest respectability may fail of being plastic.

I didn't owe my friends money, but I did see them again. They re-appeared together, three days later, and under the circumstances there was something tragic in the fact. It was a proof to me that they could find nothing else in life to do. They had threshed the matter out in a dismal conference— they had digested the bad news that they were not in for the series. If they were not useful to me even for the *Cheapside* their function seemed difficult to determine, and I could only judge at first that they had come, forgivingly, decorously, to take a last leave. This made me rejoice in secret that I had little leisure for a scene; for I had placed both my other models in position together and I was pegging away at a drawing from which I hoped to derive glory. It had been suggested by the passage in which Rutland Ramsay, drawing up a chair to Artemisia's piano-stool, says extraordinary things to her while she ostensibly fingers out a difficult piece of music. I had done Miss Churm at the piano before—it was an attitude in which she knew how to take on an absolutely poetic grace. I wished the two figures to "compose" together, intensely, and my little Italian had entered perfectly into my conception. The pair were vividly before me, the piano had been pulled out; it was a charming picture of blended youth and murmured love, which I had only to catch and keep. My visitors stood and looked at it, and I was friendly to them over my shoulder.

They made no response, but I was used to silent company and went on with my work, only a little disconcerted (even though exhilarated by the sense that *this* was at least the ideal thing), at not having got rid of them after all. Presently I heard Mrs. Monarch's sweet voice beside, or rather above me: "I wish her hair was a little better done." I looked up and she was staring with a strange fixedness at Miss Churm, whose back was turned to her. "Do you mind my just touching it?" she went on—a question which made me spring up for an instant, as with the instinctive fear that she might do the young lady a harm. But she quieted me with a glance I shall never forget—I confess I should like to have been able to paint *that*—and went for a moment to my model. She spoke to her softly, laying a hand upon her shoulder and bending over her; and as the girl, understanding, gratefully assented, she disposed her rough curls, with a few quick passes, in such a way as to make Miss Churm's head twice as charming. It was one of the most heroic personal services I have ever seen rendered. Then Mrs. Monarch turned away with a low sigh and, looking about her as if for something to do, stooped to the floor with a noble humility and picked up a dirty rag that had dropped out of my paint-box.

The Major meanwhile had also been looking for something to do and, wandering to the other end of the studio, saw before him my breakfast things, neglected, unremoved. "I say, can't I be useful *here?*" he called out to me with an irrepressible quaver. I assented with a laugh that I fear was awkward and for the next ten minutes, while I worked, I heard the light clatter of china and the tinkle of spoons and glass. Mrs. Monarch assisted her husband—they washed up my crockery, they put it away. They wandered off into my little scullery, and I afterwards found that they had cleaned my knives and that my slender stock of plate had an unprecedented surface. When it came over me, the latent eloquence of what they were doing, I confess that my drawing was blurred for a moment—the picture swam. They had accepted their failure, but they couldn't accept their fate. They had bowed their heads in bewilderment to the perverse and cruel law in virtue of which the real thing could be so much less precious than the unreal; but they didn't want to starve. If my servants were my models, my models might be my servants. They would reverse the parts— the others would sit for the ladies and gentlemen, and *they* would do the work. They would still be in the studio—it was an intense dumb appeal to me not to turn them out. "Take us on," they wanted to say—"we'll do *anything*."

When all this hung before me the *afflatus* vanished—my pencil dropped from my hand. My sitting was spoiled and I got rid of my sitters, who were also evidently rather mystified and awestruck. Then, alone with the Major and his wife, I had a most uncomfortable moment. He put their prayer into a single sentence: "I say, you know—just let *us* do for you, can't you?" I couldn't—it was dreadful to see them emptying my slops; but I pretended I could, to oblige them, for about a week. Then I gave them a sum of money to go away; and I never saw them again. I obtained the remaining books, but my friend Hawley repeats that Major and Mrs. Monarch did me a permanent harm, got me into a second-rate trick. If it be true I am content to have paid the price—for the memory.

WHAT IS ART FICTION?

The intersection of art and life. Painting with words. Portmay Press brings contemporary and classic works of art fiction to a wide readership.

OTHER TITLES OF INTEREST FROM PORTMAY PRESS

Art Fiction: Stories
Edited by Genevieve Sheets

Art Fiction Stories II
Edited by Ellen Francese

Marriage of the Smila-Hoffmans
Maryann D'Agincourt

The Painted Veil
W. Somerset Maugham

Night and Day
Virginia Woolf

Washington Square
Henry James

www.ingramcontent.com/pod-product-compliance
Lightning Source LLC
Chambersburg PA
CBHW022108050726
47591CB00002B/725